D0842544

TIME FOR KIDS®

BEGINNING 1 READER — *Science Scoops*

Bears!

By the Editors of TIME For Kids
WITH NICOLE IORIO

HarperCollins*Publishers*

About the Author: Nicole Iorio has been educating children for more than a decade, as a teacher and as an editor at TIME FOR KIDS®. She is also the author of the TIME FOR KIDS® Science Scoops books *BATS!* and *SPIDERS!* She lives in New York with her husband and son.

To my mom, Eileen, who takes such good care of all her cubs

Thanks to Stephanie Simek, Bear Management, Florida Fish and Wildlife Commission   —N.I.

Library of Congress Cataloging-in-Publication Data is available.
ISBN 0-06-078196-3 (pbk.) — ISBN 0-06-078201-3 (trade)

1 2 3 4 5 6 7 8 9 10
First Edition

Photography and Illustration Credits:
Cover: Pete Oxford—Minden; cover insert: Thomas Mangelsen—Minden; cover flap: Kevin Schafer; title page: John Hyde; pg. 3: Tui De Roy—Minden; pp. 4–5: Robert Sabin—Animals Animals; pp. 6–7: Ron Magill; pp. 8–9: Digital Vision; pg. 9 (inset): Barbara Spurll; pp. 10–11: William Munoz; pp. 12–13: Mark Newman—Photo Researchers; pp. 14–15: Keren Su—Corbis; pp. 16–17: Claro Cortes—Reuters; pp. 18–19: Erwin & Peggy Bauer—Bruce Coleman; pp. 20–21: Ingram Publishing/Alamy; pp. 22–23: Patricio Roblen Gil—Sierra Madre/Minden; pp. 24–25: W. Perry Conway—Corbis; pp. 26–27: Sumio Harada—Minden; pg. 26 (inset): John Courtney; pp. 28–29: Fred Whitehead—Animals Animals; pp. 30–31: Renee Lynn—Corbis; pg. 32 (claws): Claro Cortes—Reuters; pg. 32 (cub): Mark Newman—Photo Researchers; pg. 32 (den): Fred Whitehead—Animals Animals; pg. 32 (fur): Sumio Harada—Minden; pg. 32 (mammal): Keren Su—Corbis; pg. 32 (paws): ZSSD/Superstock

Bears Pictured:
Cover: panda bear; cover insert: brown bear; cover flap: polar bear; title page: brown bear; pg. 3: spectacled bear; pp. 4–5: brown bear; pp. 6–7: sloth bear; pp. 8–9: polar bear; pp. 10–11: sun bear; pp. 12–13: brown bear; pp. 14–15: panda bear; pp. 16–17: Asiatic black bear; pp. 18–19: sun bear; pp. 20–21: panda bear; pp. 22–23: polar bear; pp. 24–25: brown bear; pp. 26–27: American black bear; pp. 28–29: American black bear; pp. 30–31: American black bear

Acknowledgments:
For TIME FOR KIDS: Editorial Director: Keith Garton; Editor: Nelida Gonzalez Cutler; Art Director: Rachel Smith; Photography Editor: Jill Tatara

 Check us out at www.timeforkids.com

Deep in the woods,
bears have busy days.

Bears can run very fast.
They can swim for hours.

Bears are mammals.
All bears have hair called fur.
It can be black, brown, or tan.
It can even be white or silvery blue.

Bears are different sizes.
Polar bears are huge.
They can be ten feet tall
when they stand.

That Is Amazing!

A polar bear is too tall to stand inside a house!

Sun bears are the smallest bears. They are only about four feet tall when they stand.

Baby bears are tiny when
they are born.
But they grow fast!
Baby bears are called cubs.

Cubs need their mothers.
Cubs drink milk from their mothers.
Mother bears keep cubs safe.

When bears grow up,
they leave their mothers.
They look for food on their own.

Sun bears love honey!
Their long tongues are
good for licking.
They live in rain forests.

Giant pandas eat bamboo plants.
They pull off leaves and stems
with their paws.
Pandas live only in China.

Polar bears grab seals with their sharp teeth and claws. They live near the North Pole.

Brown bears eat all kinds of food.
In the summer, some go fishing!
They live in many parts of the world.

That Is Amazing!

In one day, a bear in the wild can eat as much food as 42 hamburgers.

Many bears eat all summer and fall.
They must store up fat for a cold winter.

In the late fall, many bears
find winter homes.
Their homes are called dens.
These bears do not eat, drink,
or move about all winter.

Cubs are born in the winter.
In the spring, they come out to play!
They see a new, colorful world.

WORDS to Know

Claws:
sharp nails
on paws

Fur:
the hairy
coat on an
animal

Cub:
a baby
bear

Mammal:
an animal that
has hair and
drinks milk
from its
mother

Den:
a bear's
home

Paws:
a bear's feet